This book belongs to

LINNIE VON SKY

Sadly
the Owl

AN UNTOLD TALE

illustrations by
ASHLEY O'MARA

Silk Web Publishing

When the **first ray** of golden sun danced into his nest and tickled his beak, Sadly the owl opened his eyes, threw back the covers, and **jumped** out of bed into his **flaming red** line-dancing **boots**.

Like every morning, Sadly took extra care to preen his feathers and wings. Most importantly, **he polished his boots** until they **gleamed** in the prairie sunshine. They were his **pride and joy**.

After his puddle bath, Sadly hit the play button on his **favourite** country music station and before long he was **clicking** his heels and **bobbing** his head as he floated to the table on the scrumptious scent waves of mom's crunchy **cricket pancakes**.

There was only one thing Sadly **loved more** than his shiny red line-dancing boots, and that was to **stride through** the swinging wooden doors of the saloon and onto the dance floor where he ....

flexed, flicked,
and fanned

while he hopped,
heel split, and hee-hawed.

Try
Canadian

Ginger Ale

Then, one morning,
everything changed.

When Sadly opened his pearly owl eyes, he saw a
dark cloud hovering directly over his head . When
he slipped on his boots
to step into the sun's rays,
the **cloud floated along**
above his head.

In the coming days Sadly **tried every trick** under the sun to outsmart his cloud. He hid under his bed, but the cloud waited. He skipped to the left, but **the cloud followed**. He swung open the saloon doors hoping to bat the cloud away, but it simply swooshed through the wooden cracks and settled **back over his head**.

The **cloud** had no intention of leaving and the **harder Sadly worked** to outsmart it, the darker it grew until one day it began raining big **splish-splash raindrops** down on little Sadly's head.

The nest bell rang again and again as his friends begged Sadly to join in their **fun**. Instead of answering their pleas, poor Sadly pulled the covers **over his head**. What was the point if his boots no longer sparkled, his heels were **too tired** to click, and his wings were **too wet** to clap?

Seeing Sadly **sooo sad**, mom phoned the **wise old medicine owl** who immediately flew over with his heavy bag of **magic potions**.

He inspected Sadly's **muddy red cowboy boots**, poked the cloud and bounced it around, tasted a raindrop, and **dried Sadly's tears**. He straightened his thick horn glasses before raising his wise, deep voice.

"**Every day** Sadly must open one of the **six notes** I will leave at his bedside." And with that he spread his wings and leapt out of the nest, leaving Sadly (and mom) filled with a **sprinkle of hope** that things might finally get brighter.

On Monday morning Sadly opened a note and read:

Wise Owl
family practice

Monday,

Receive a heartfelt cuddle from someone you love and who loves you in return.

From the desk of: Ken Wise.

Although he felt **weak, wobbly, and whiney**, he **dragged** himself over to mom for a heartfelt cuddle. He sure loved his mommy and he was sure **she loved him** more than any owl under the prairie sun. She also didn't mind getting wet as a few of Sadly's **raindrops dampened** her feather dress.

After they hugged, Sadly curiously peeked up at his cloud to find that although it had not moved, it was **a little less puffy**.

On Tuesday morning Sadly opened a note
and read:

Tuesday,

    Leave your nest
      and seek the sunlight.

From the desk of:
KenWise.

Although he felt **gloomy, grey, and groggy,** Sadly hopped around his neighborhood. He saw the other animals bathing in the **sunshine** and remembered **what life looked like** before his cloud appeared.

After his prairie hop, Sadly curiously peeked up at his cloud to find that although it had not moved, it seemed **a little lighter.**

On Wednesday morning Sadly opened a note
and read:

WISE OWL
family practice

Wednesday,
    Go to the market and
    prepare yourself your
    favourite meal.

From the desk of: *Ken Wise.*

Although he felt **mopey, messy, and muddled**, he joined mom at the market where they bought cricket salad, **worm tapenade**, and bat steak. They prepared a lovely feast and Sadly remembered **what life tasted like** before his cloud appeared.

After dinner, Sadly curiously peeked up at his cloud to find that although it had not moved, it did **rain a little less**.

On Thursday morning Sadly opened a note and read:

WISE OWL
family practice

Thursday,
    Play until your
        feathers are fluffed.

From the desk of:
KenWise.

Although he felt **dull, daft, and drowsy**, he joined his friends on the ski hill where his cloud's rain **turned to snow** and Sadly remembered **what life felt like** before his cloud appeared.

After his ski adventure, Sadly **curiously** peeked up at his cloud to find that although it had not moved, it was **a little more see-through**.

On Friday morning Sadly opened a note and read:

WISE OWL
family practice

Friday,
　　Do something that makes you forget your cloud.

From the desk of:
Ken Wise.

Although he felt **overwhelmed, overwrought, and on his own**, he volunteered to play with the pre-school owls at the big puddle pond. The little owls' **giggly hoots** filled the prairie air and Sadly remembered **what life sounded like** before his cloud appeared.

After his day at the **puddle pond**, Sadly curiously peeked up at his cloud to find that although it had not moved, it did look **a little smaller.**

On Saturday morning Sadly opened a note and read:

WISE OWL
family practice

Saturday.

Repeat all the lovely things you did this week and tonight, when you go to bed, let your mommy tuck you in and count the stars until you sleep, sleep, sleep.

From the desk of:
KenWise.

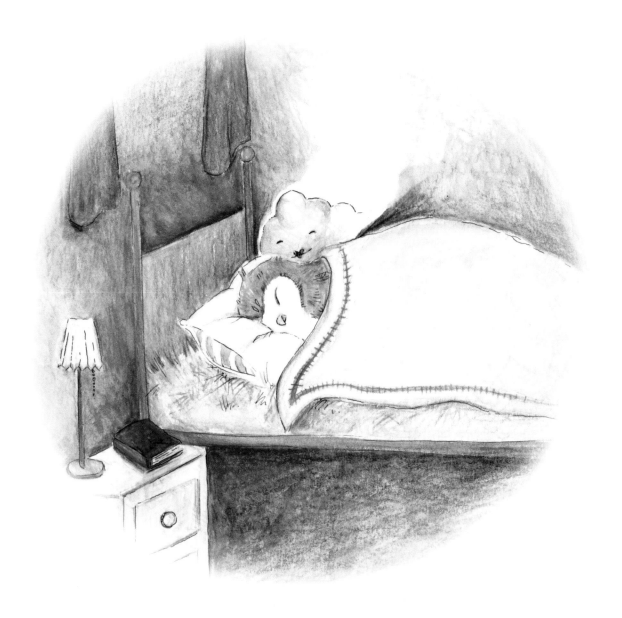

That night Sadly was so sound asleep that he didn't notice the **cloud kissing him good-bye**. Before leaving, it poured a final shower over his **favourite red line-dancing boots** so they would once again gleam in the **prairie sun**.

The **Happy End*** (for now)

*that every little owl deserves

Sadly's cloud has visited me one too many times. I feel deep gratitude that my loving family held me through each and every episode and continues to monitor my mental wellbeing. It is the greatest gift to have recovered my health to become a loving wife to my darling Nicolas and mother to my sweet fairy Ella Élise. I hope Sadly sparks a conversation. ~ Linnie

I, and many of my friends and family can relate to what Sadly the Owl goes through in this story. I'm so happy to be a part of this book to start a conversation between children and their parents. Thank you to my family, my lovely husband, Mike, our two soft kitties, and of course, Linnie, for believing in me. ~ Ashley

Sadly the owl loves nothing more than line-dancing in his bright red cowboy boots. One morning Sadly wakes up to find a dark cloud over his head. He tries every trick he knows to get back into the sunshine, but nothing works. Will Sadly ever get to dance again? A tale about more than just sad days.

First published in hardback in Canada by Silk Web Publishing in 2015

Text and illustration copyright © 2015 by Linnie von Sky.
Illustrated by Ashley O'Mara - Ashley hand-illustrated Sadly the Owl in water colour pencil crayon.

Type is set in Cassia and LunchBox.

Printed and bound by Friesens in Altona, Canada on FSC ® certified paper using vegetable-based ink.

Cataloging data available from Library and Archives Canada.

ISBN 978-0-9919612-2-1 (bound)

Author: Linnie von Sky; Illustrator: Ashley O'Mara; Editor: Taisha Garby; Book Designer: Ashley O'Mara
Digitalization of Ashley's original drawings magically done by Imagine This Photographics Inc.

This is a testament to the awesomeness of those who made our third publishing dream fly:
My mother Christine and papa Arya for believing in me from the very beginning. The Leuie Ladies for their prayers, love, and support. Amie Gutierrez for being a fellow dreamer and dear friend. SJ for being our adopted family member and international man of leisure and travel who distributes our work with such enthusiasm.

Introducing the custom characters and an extra sprinkle of gratitude:
Sophie the horse for Scott's darling daughter Sophie.
The elephant caravan for Jenn, Sean, and darling Maddi.
The "hang in there" cat for Julie and Ron's darling granddaughter Arianna.
Captain Squeezy the squirrel for my darling husband Nicolas.
Llama llama for papa Arya.
Buffy the red robin for Jancis O'Mara.
The Mwangi Moose for the newlyweds Rashmi and Kevin Mwangi, my darling brother and sister.
Willie the donkey for Mama Tini.

FSC
www.fsc.org

MIX
Paper from responsible sources
FSC® C016245